DINER DOGS

by Eric Seltzer
illustrated by Tom Disbury

Ready-to-Read

Simon Spotlight

New York   London   Toronto   Sydney   New Delhi

In loving memory of
my Aunt Ginny and Uncle Ray Sharkey —E. S.

For my dear dog, Wilma —T. D.

SIMON SPOTLIGHT
An imprint of Simon & Schuster Children's Publishing Division
1230 Avenue of the Americas, New York, New York 10020
This Simon Spotlight edition July 2021
Text copyright © 2021 by Eric Seltzer
Illustrations copyright © 2021 by Tom Disbury
All rights reserved, including the right of reproduction in whole
or in part in any form.
SIMON SPOTLIGHT, READY-TO-READ, and colophon are registered
trademarks of Simon & Schuster, Inc.
For information about special discounts for bulk purchases, please contact
Simon & Schuster Special Sales at 1-866-506-1949
or business@simonandschuster.com.
Manufactured in the United States of America 0621 LAK
2 4 6 8 10 9 7 5 3 1
The book has been cataloged with the Library of Congress.
ISBN 978-1-5344-9386-5 (hc)
ISBN 978-1-5344-9385-8 (pbk)
ISBN 978-1-5344-9387-2 (eBook)

Diner dogs all
wake with a grin.

Soon it will be
time to begin!

Diner dogs start
with belly rubs.

Diner dogs scrub
with soap in tubs.

Diner dogs like
to roll over.

Just ask Ace and
Duke and Grover.

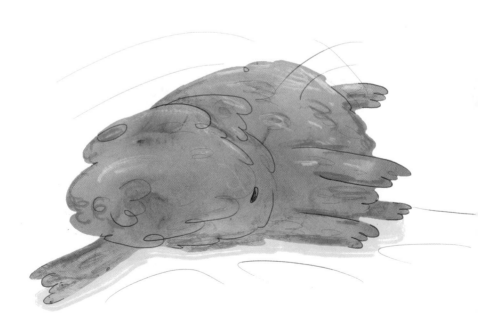

Then they open
the diner door.

Diner dogs fetch . . .
cups, plates, and more!

Diner dogs make
batter and dough.

Now they are
all set to go.

They make hot dogs.

They make French fries.

They bake pound cakes
and apple pies.

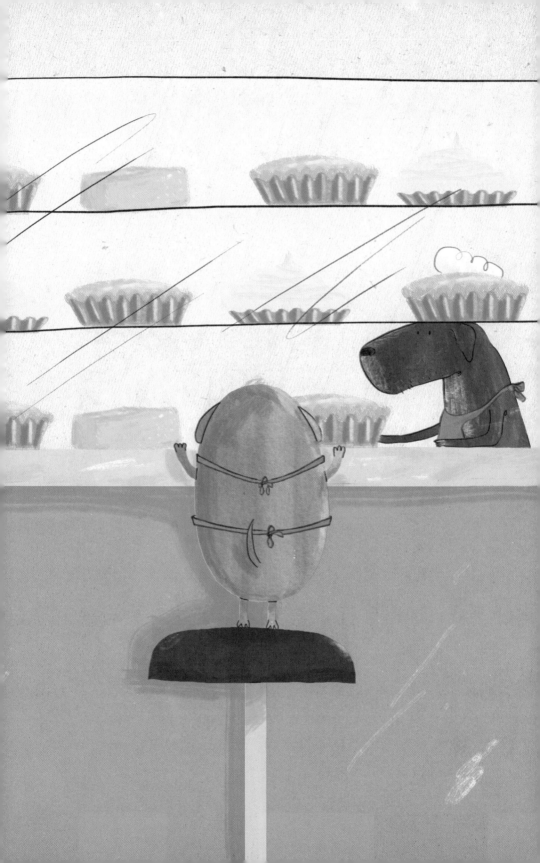

Diner dogs serve
bowls of chili . . .

to Spot and Dot,
Rex and Millie.

Diner dogs fill

mugs and teacups . . .

with some help from
the diner pups.

Here come space cows.
They want French toast.

Party pigs like
pancakes the most.

Then it is time
to clean up shop.

Diner dogs dance,
wipe, sweep, and mop!

The diner dog
workday is done.

Bow Wow has chow
for everyone!